RAT KING

OLIVIA GRATEHOUSE

Copyright © 2025 by Olivia Gratehouse

All rights reserved. No part of this book may be reproduced, distributed, or transmitted in an form or by any means, including photocopying, recording, or other electronic or mechanical methods, without the express written permission of the author, except in the case of brief quotations embodied in critical reviews or other non-commercial uses permitted by copyright law.

Readers seeking distribution within the goblin realm must also have express permission from the Society of Darkening Overlords.

This is a work of fiction. Names, characters, incidents, and dialogues bearing any resemblance to actual events or persons, living or dead, is entirely coincidental.

NO AI TRAINING. Without any limitation on the author or by Olivia Gratehouse's exclusive copyright rights, any use of this publication to train generative artificial intelligence is expressly forbidden.

Contents

1. Chapter One   3
2. Chapter Two   12
3. Chapter Three   19
4. Chapter Four   25
5. Chapter Five   31
6. Chapter Six   40
7. Chapter Seven   53
8. Chapter Eight   70
About the Author   89

*For the Overcomers, who helped me bring Rat King to life.
Thanks for the magnificent hat. ;)*

*And for Allison and Emily.
Thanks for rekindling my love for goblins.*

Chapter One

Working as a grunt in a Dark Lady's army wasn't the worst job in the world. It wasn't the best one either. (Don't tell her I said that!)

But it's not like goblins had a say-so in these matters. We usually moped around in our swamps until a Dark Lord or Lady came and inducted us into their armies. Then we just stuck to whoever was biggest, strongest, and fed us the most grub.

Lady Amaryl, Vampire Queen of the Goblin Horde, was mean, bossy, scary, and a little more glamorous a boss than we goblins were used to working for. But the nice thing about her was that she didn't kill us grunts when she got mad. (I'd heard the horror stories. What kinda monster killed their own employees?)

As it turned out, she didn't do much more than sleep in her coffin, fiddle with her poisons, and lure dashing Adventurers to their demise. But that meant our job was easy: all we had to do was stand guard, defend the chateau, and surrender our lives in glorious battle when the Dark Lady inevitably rose to power. No biggie.

But until that day arrived, I was stuck with the slowest, most boring job in all the castle.

Inventory.

It started like any normal weeknight at the Chateau l'Amaryl: with me sweeping the storeroom floors and making the final count for tomorrow's delivery. At least, that was how my night had *started*. Right now, I was at a standoff with one of the deadliest monsters known to goblinkind: *a cat.*

The big orange tabby hissed at me, and I hissed right back, holding my ground—and my broom—at the ready. Between us hunched a rat. *My* rat, her white fur bristled in fear. She held something in her mouth that I couldn't see, but I knew must be important. Windtail wouldn't've risked rankling the beast if it weren't.

The three of us stood frozen, eyeing each other across the distance. The cat hunkered low, eyes wide, tail twitching. One wrong move, and it'd be on Windtail in a heartbeat. I couldn't let that happen!

Then a clap of thunder boomed outside the window, and it broke the spell.

Windtail squealed and bounded toward me. The cat yowled and leapt at her. I snarled and brandished my broom. The bristles clipped the cat's tail, and the little beast pivoted just as Windtail scrambled up my leg and into my pocket. The cat sank its claws into my ankles, and I beat at it with my broom, whacking myself in the process.

Hissing, the beast released me and dashed to the other side of the room. Its wild eyes told me it hadn't given up, so I yelled and ran at it, waving the broom like a club until, with a shriek, the animal tore past me and disappeared out the door.

"That's right, you toadbrain!" I spat. "Scram!"

I held the broom up for the span of five breaths, then sighed and lowered it back to the floor.

Windtail trembled in my trouser pocket, and I gently rested a hand over her tiny body.

"It's alright," I whispered. "That monster's gone."

Tentatively, Windtail peeked her head out and looked around before scrambling up to my shoulder. She still held something in her mouth, and when I held up my hand, she dropped it onto my palm.

"Whaddya find this time?"

It was a rock, not much bigger than my thumb, and an unusual shade of blue, speckled with white. It was so pretty, it could've passed for a tiny dragon egg, and I couldn't contain my excitement.

"Windtail!" I gasped. "This is beautiful!"

The rat stood on her hind legs, nose twitching with pleasure.

Reaching into my other pocket, I hurried over to a table in the corner and dumped the contents on the surface. Five more rocks rolled onto the worn wood with a clatter, and I added the blue one, sorting them by size. It was the prettiest by far, so colorful next to the others. There was a flat one, a triangle one, a black one, one shaped like an elf ear, and a large, smooth one nearly as big as my fist.

I smiled down at the treasures we'd gathered over the last few weeks. "These are wonderful, Windtail! I just know Jab will love them!" Truthfully, Jab loved any rock, no matter how unremarkable I thought it was. But he always seemed so pleased when I found one for him, so it made the hunt worth it in the end.

The back door abruptly banged open with a flash of thunder and lightning, and I jumped and whirled around as Windtail darted back into my pocket.

"Who's there?" I demanded. "No one's s'posed to—"

But I stopped short as I beheld the most magnificent hat I'd ever seen: brown and wide-brimmed, and though it dripped with rainwater, a plume of orange phoenix feathers sprouted from the back, flickering and sparking with magic fire.

I sighed longingly. Oh, the way it taunted me, that remarkable hat....

"Where's Amaryl?"

The hat-wearer spoke in a deep, clipped voice, and I reluctantly tore my gaze down to the human beneath it. Tall and slender, Captain Teagan's green eyes bored into me with a deep intensity.

"Well?" he prompted. "Can you answer me or not?"

My mouth went dry. Captain Teagan was talking to *me*? A lowly grunt? This just might've been the best day of my life!

Quickly, I formed the salute I'd seen his crew do so often.

"Sir!" I said. "Since it's sundown, she probably just woke up and went to the throne room!"

The captain smirked, and I wondered if the salute pleased him. What had brought him here at this hour, anyway? Lady Amaryl's poison ingredients weren't due for delivery until the morning, and it was always a troll that brought them.

The human stared at me with a curious expression I couldn't make out. Humans were weird like that, faces scrunching up in hard-to-read ways. Finally, he smiled (and smiles I *could* read).

"Won't you show me the way to the throne room?" he asked.

I blinked, then stood a little straighter. "Yes, sir! Right away, sir!" Wow, Teagan needed *my* help! *The* Captain Teagan!

Quick as I could, I set my broom against a shelf and darted to the door, opening it wide and allowing Captain Teagan to pass through first.

It was a long walk to the throne room, so I didn't know why Teagan couldn't have just taken the chateau's main entrance. But the captain didn't complain, walking so fast that I had to jog to keep up. We passed by the kitchens, where the smell of breakfast made my mouth water. But I moved with a purpose, winding through halls till at last we reached the entrance to the throne room. Two goblin guards stood at attention, glaring at Teagan as we approached.

"Thank you," Teagan said. "I'll take it from here."

"I dunno," I gasped, out of breath from the exertion. "At least let me announce—"

But the captain was already swaggering forward, and with an internal groan I ambled after him. The guards jumped to life as Teagan approached and crossed their spears.

"No entrance unless Lady Amaryl allows it!" said one.

"Don't worry," Teagan said. "She'll allow me."

"That's not—" began the other. But before I could even blink, Teagan flicked his wrist and summoned a long strand of...was it dark? Light? Dark-light? Whatever it was, I could tell it was magic by the way it made the air ripple. Teagan wielded the dark-light like a whip, wrapping it around one guard's neck as he kicked the other to the ground. And in a matter of seconds, the two goblins were out cold.

Then Teagan pushed through the giant oak doors, and they creaked shrilly on their hinges. I winced, looking with concern at the fallen guards. They were still unconscious, thank the swamps, and I didn't want to stick around for when they woke up and started casting blame on the nearest hapless grunt. So, hunching my shoulders, I hurried after Teagan, doing my best to stay behind him.

Lady Amaryl was on her throne, swirling a crystal goblet full of red liquid. She was an imposing woman, with ashen skin, raven hair, and lips as red as blood. Quite the formidable boss.

She looked up at the sound of our entrance and made a strange face, then flashed a bright smile that showed off her venomous fangs.

"Captain Teagan!" she called, her voice like fine music. "*However* did you manage to get in here?"

Teagan came to a halt before the dais and swept off his gorgeous hat with a shower of orange sparks. "Through a back entrance, my lady. You really ought to consider a higher security detail. Why, *any* old riffraff could come waltzing in."

"I see." Lady Amaryl's eyes flickered to me, and I cowered under her deadly gaze. With a sigh, she leaned back on her throne and crossed her legs, lifting her goblet once again. "And to what do I owe the pleasure? We weren't expecting your delivery until tomorrow."

"Delivery will be on time," Teagan answered coolly. "However, I wish to speak to you on another matter." His smile grew wider. "How much do you know about the wizard lord, Dari Varyon?"

Lady Amaryl sat up straight, choking on her drink. "*The* Lord Varyon?" she gasped, narrowing her eyes at Teagan. "Yes, Lord Varyon is an old...*acquaintance* of mine. But I haven't spoken with him in...oh, *an age.*" She took a sip of her drink. "I hope you aren't looking for a referral...Varyon and I...well, we didn't part on the best of terms."

"No need," Teagan answered. "I already work with the wizard: delivering cargo, just like I do for you."

"Indeed." Lady Amaryl pursed her lips. "Then what could you possibly want with me?"

"More like...what do I want *from* you." Teagan grinned. "I have a proposition—a way to kill two birds with one stone. A *Seeing Stone*, you might say."

Lady Amaryl's eyes grew wide and, for a moment, all she did was stare. Then she gave a wicked smile and rose from her throne, sauntering down the dais until she stood before the captain.

"Well then," she said, slipping her arm through his. "I'm sure I'll love to hear all about it."

She paused and turned her gaze back on me.

"Goblin!" she cried, and I jumped back, trembling. "Return to your duties!"

"Yes, my lady!" I said quickly, bowing so low my ears grazed the floor. I backed out of the room as fast as I could, but by the time I was out the door, the two guards were starting to wake, so I ran down the hall until they were out of sight.

I leaned against a wall, heart pounding, and took a moment to catch my breath. Then I forced my way onward, walking back to the storerooms at a more reasonable pace. When I reached my work station, it suddenly felt big and empty.

I sighed, wishing I could've listened in on the conversation. Teagan was probably recounting some of his awesome adventures to Lady Amaryl, and that must have been why she was so eager to talk to him. I leaned against a work table, propping my chin in my hands. I *so* wanted to go on adventures like Captain Teagan did. To explore the great unknown and see all the world had to offer....

But it would never happen. Grunts like me never did *anything* fun.

I glanced down at the table and found the collection of stones still spread out on the worn surface. The bright blue dragon-y stone glimmered in the low light, and I picked it up. Windtail took the opportunity to climb from my pocket and settle onto my shoulder, gently nuzzling my ear. I scratched her head with one hand and sorted through the stones again with the other. At the very least, I could give these to Jab, and he could tell me all about *his* adventures.

Sweeping the stones off the table and into my pocket, I took up my broom again. There was still a lot of work to be done before delivery.

Chapter Two

The next morning was cool and smelled wet after the storm. The sun hadn't yet risen, making the sleeping chateau more peaceful, so I spent a few minutes picking worms from the cobblestone for a late snack. I yawned, looking forward to retiring for the day after squaring away the delivery.

I sat on a rain barrel with my back to the chateau's stone wall, kicking my feet as I waited and munched on the worms. It was a long walk from here to the ocean, so I didn't know how long it'd be.

I'd never seen the ocean. My bond to Lady Amaryl's service kept me from leaving her domain, so I couldn't travel far. But Jab said the ocean was the biggest water ever, which was hard to imagine. It sounded so *adventurous*.

My snack was almost gone by the time I heard the squeak of wheels, and I sat up straighter, ears twitching as I listened. Even Windtail seemed excited, hopping down from my shoulder to perch on the rain barrel.

I held my breath, silently pleading as I watched the shadow emerge from the darkness. Then I couldn't contain my grin as the gigantic mountain troll came to a halt before me.

"Jab!" I cried, jumping to my feet. "It's you!"

The troll gave me a lopsided smile, then reached out and slammed his palm twice over the top of my head. Stars exploded in my vision, and I fell back against the chateau wall, vision swimming, head pounding. But my smile remained as I clambered back to my feet.

Even standing on the barrel, my head barely reached Jab's waist. (I wasn't bitter about that or anything.) He was about as broad and heavy as the mountains he came from, with long arms that reached past his knees and gray skin that was rough like stone. Everything about him was gray—his skin, his scraggly hair, his big teeth—everything except his enormous eyes, which were a piercing blue.

He was slow, like all mountain trolls, but his strength was unmatched as he began lifting crates from his wagon and stacking them next to the door.

"I'm *so* glad it's you and not Bash!" I said, bouncing on the balls of my feet. "Last month he was so rude! He wouldn't even talk to me, and he put the crates in the wrong room! I had to spend all day dragging the sacks one by one into the storerooms!"

Jab grunted in sympathy at his brother's laziness. When the wagon was empty, he pulled two of the shipping crates onto his shoulders, and I hurried to open the door, flattening myself against a wall as Jab squeezed his way through.

He clomped forward, each footstep making the walls shake, and I darted under his legs and rushed to reach the storeroom first, opening the door and holding it wide so the troll could duck inside. He dropped the crates on the floor, sending a cloud of powder and spices into the air. I sneezed, nose and throat burning, but stumbled my way out again, Jab close behind.

"I wanna hear all about your travels!" I said, as we headed back to the door. "Did you go anywhere interesting this time?"

Jab paused, a giant hand pressed against his chin in thought. Then he smiled and stretched his arm up as high as it would go, knuckles bumping into the ceiling.

"Uhhh," I said as we slipped back outside. I tried to think of what would be so tall. "A tree? Ohhh...a wizard's tower?"

Jab shook his head, then snapped his fingers. Lifting both his arms above his head, he touched his fingers together and bent his elbows, making a triangle.

"Oh!" I cried. "You went to a mountain!"

Jab nodded enthusiastically, grabbing another armload of crates.

"Were they your home mountains?"

Jab shook his head and shrugged.

"Just ordinary mountains then. Still, that sounds amazing! Wish I coulda seen them for myself."

RAT KING 15

Jab was the strong, silent type. To be honest, I didn't know if "Jab" was even his real name, but when I'd asked, he'd made pokey-sticky-jabbing motions with his club. So that's what I'd called him, and he never told me elsewise. (I think it must've been a troll thing, 'cause his brother Bash didn't speak neither: just pointed and grunted. But over the years I'd learned to understand Jab-speech, and we'd gotten pretty good at conversations.)

When we were finally done unloading, the sun was just starting to brighten the sky, so we sat outside and enjoyed the morning air.

"Oh!" I burst out. "I almost forgot: we got you more rocks!"

I fished out the handful I'd been saving up. "There's some frog-rotting good ones in here if I do say so myself! Lots of neat shapes, and Windtail found one that looks like a tiny dragon egg!"

Jab held out his hand and I dropped the stones onto his palm, saving the dragon-y stone for last. Windtail hopped down from my shoulder and scurried onto Jab's, watching as he mixed the stones around in his hand, admiring them in the new light. Of course he went for the dragon-y stone first, grinning broadly as he turned it over in his hands. He tossed it up and down in his palm, then bit on it gently before admiring it once again.

"Isn't it beautiful?" I exclaimed.

The troll turned to me with a huge smile, then reached into his own pocket and withdrew a small package. He stuffed it into my hands, and I immediately caught a whiff of something sweet.

Mouth watering, I reached into the package and withdrew some kind of fruit that probably used to be round, but was now flat after sitting in Jab's pocket. Crushed and sticky, the overripe food smelled *so* good.

I took an eager bite and was overwhelmed by the bittersweet flavor.

"Oh *wow!*" I cried, flecking juice onto my chin. I'd never tasted this kind of fruit before. I ate the whole thing in just a few bites until all that was left was a pit, which I gobbled down as well.

I looked into the bag and saw three more pieces of crushed fruit, and was tempted to finish off the contents then and there. But I wanted to savor these, so I closed the bag again and stuffed it into my pocket, feeling the way the fruit squished between the paper.

"Man," I said, wiping my mouth on my sleeve and my hands on my trousers. "You always find the best food. I wish I could eat like that every day!"

Jab paused, looking up from the stones to me, and his face broke into a huge smile, broader than I'd ever seen it before. He pointed to me, then turned and pointed over his shoulder, toward the sea beyond Lady Amaryl's domain.

I blinked, trying to gather his meaning. "What, me...go with you?" I shook my head. "You know I'd love to, Jab. Going on an adventure with you would be a dream come true! But the boss would never let me go."

Jab shrugged, then lifted his hand and made a wide, circling motion around his head before pointing to me again. I just stared at him, aware of only one person who would wear such a large and fantastic hat.

"Teagan?" I guessed. "Captain Teagan?"

Jab nodded excitedly and pointed to me, then to himself, then again to the sea.

"He's..." I hardly dared to say it. "He wants to...*hire me?*"

Jab made a tilting motion with his hand.

"Not me specifically," I guessed, "but one of us goblins?"

Jab nodded again, clapping.

I slumped backwards on my barrel, pressing a hand against my forehead.

"Sweet frog-rot!" I gasped. "This could be my chance!" Is that what Teagan and Lady Amaryl had been talking about last night? I looked at Jab. "Did he say what the job was?"

Jab shrugged before returning to his rocks, but my head was spinning as if the troll had smacked me all over again.

Teagan was hiring one of us! I'd admired the human captain for as long as he and Lady Amaryl had done business together. Not only did he have impressive taste in hats, but he was also an impressive man—all posh and refined, with a ship and a crew and the whole wide world to explore. I'd always wished I could travel like him and Jab, but I was bound to Lady Amaryl. I could never leave.

I fingered the slave brand on the back of my neck. It had been there as long as I could remember—like a clamp around my soul that kept me in Lady Amaryl's service. Jab had one too, binding him to Teagan, though I wondered if the captain's brand allowed the freedom I desperately wanted.

I knew right then that I *had* to be the goblin to get that job. Someway, somehow, I *had* to make Teagan pick me.

We sat awhile in companionable silence, until Jab finally pushed to his feet. The sun had fully risen now, and it was time for the troll to return to his ship.

He held a fist out toward me, and I quickly made a fist of my own before slamming it on top of his. Windtail ran up the length of our arms to rest again on my shoulder.

"Safe travels, friend!" I said. "Maybe we'll see each other again soon?"

Jab nodded eagerly, then took up reins on his wagon and pulled it along as he headed back to his ship.

Chapter Three

I was hurrying back through the halls of the chateau, eager to turn in for the day, when a large, brown rat scampered up toward me. I froze, then peered around, worried that horrible cat might be on the prowl again. But the rat didn't seem agitated, so I lowered myself to one knee, making clicking noises with my tongue.

"Here, boy!" I said, holding out a hand.

The rat hesitated, nose twitching, before creeping forward. It sniffed my hand, whiskers tickling my fingers, then stepped onto my palm and allowed me to stroke its fur.

"What brings you all the way out here?" I said, standing up again. "We need to get you somewhere safe, before Lady Amaryl sees you! She doesn't like rats in her chateau, which is a tragedy if you ask..."

I trailed off, because the rat had suddenly turned around, pointing its nose straight ahead. I followed its gaze, confused, as I stared down the hallway.

"What is it, boy?" I whispered.

The rat leapt from my hands and landed with a *thunk* on the floor. It glanced back at me once before darting away down the hall.

"Hey!" I cried. "Come back!" But the little rat kept running, and I realized with horror that it was heading straight for the throne room.

Panicking, I rushed after it, running down the twisting halls until, once again, I found myself at the throne room entrance. Only this time, no guards stood at the door.

That was weird—Lady Amaryl was *really* particular about guard duty.

Cautiously, I peeked inside the throne room and glimpsed dozens of goblins inside, standing at attention. Then I noticed Lady Amaryl and Teagan standing on the dais.

My chest pounded. What was happening?

I crept into the throne room, hunching and keeping to the sidelines so as not to disturb the gathering. Lady Amaryl's voice echoed in the chamber, but I couldn't focus on what she was saying.

Reaching the edge of the group, I tapped one guard on the shoulder. "What's going on?"

The guard flinched and didn't look at me as he answered, "We don't know. Lady Amaryl went on and on about safety parameters, but now she's talking about a special mission."

"What kind of mission?" I asked, hardly daring to believe.

The guard shrugged. "She says one of us will have to go with Captain Teagan."

I squeaked and bounced on the balls of my feet. This *was* it! What Jab had said was true: Teagan *was* going to choose one of us to join his crew—to join in his adventure!

My eyes fell first on Teagan's excellent hat (the phoenix feathers were looking particularly fluffy) before landing on the Dark Lady. She was addressing the guards, but I was too excited to take in her words.

Quick as I could, I elbowed my way through the crowd. No one objected. In fact, most of them looked like they didn't want to be there, and seemed almost eager to stay behind.

As soon as I was in the front though, I froze. Captain Teagan was standing right before us, looking the guards over with a critical eye. Then his gaze fell on me, and he raised an eyebrow.

I gulped, looking over my shoulder, and found that the rest of the crowd had fallen back a step, leaving me stranded in the open. *Oh frog-rot.* My chest thumped loudly, suddenly nervous.

I hunched in on myself, trying to appear smaller, but Captain Teagan smiled.

"This one will do."

My ears shot up. Had he recognized me from last night? Nearly bursting with excitement, I opened my mouth to thank him. But before I could, a dark and heavy weight wrapped around my chest and tugged me forward. *Magic.* Lady Amaryl had activated my slave brand, and my feet had no choice but to obey.

"Very well, then!" Lady Amaryl held out her hand, and the captain stepped forward and clasped his hand over her palm. A tendril of the strange dark-light burst from his fingers and wound around their wrists.

I stiffened as the slave brand on my neck flared red-hot, and something in my chest seemed to snap.

For a tiny moment, I was weightless, unattached, completely free. It felt like I could go anywhere, do anything, and no one could stop me!

Then something hit me like a rock to the face, and a soft voice, echoey and far away, called to me.

'R.K.?'

It sounded like a dream. Was it a dream? I wanted the dream-voice to say something more because it sounded nice. But then another snapping feeling brought me back to reality.

A spark of the dark-light bounced off Tegan's hand and flew straight into my neck, and I shivered as the magic fused to my slave brand.

Stunned, I lifted my fingers and lightly grazed the new, sensitive skin. Though I couldn't see it, somehow I knew it matched Jab's now.

When I looked up, Teagan was in front of me. I barely came up to his hip.

"Give me your arm," he said.

Blinking, I held up my left arm as the captain reached into his waistcoat pocket and pulled out a small vial of black liquid.

"A magic brand?" Lady Amaryl mused. "How very...*interesting*. Are you sure that's wise?"

"I am." Teagan shook the bottle and poured a drop onto his thumb. Taking my hand, he tugged me forward, and without so much as a warning, pressed his thumb into my wrist.

Pain stabbed through my skin like a knife. I gasped and tried to pull back, but Teagan's grip was like iron as he held his thumb in place.

Hot and cold shot up my arm and into my chest, swelling like a bubble and flooding me with a strange energy I'd never felt before. Suddenly everything felt clearer—sight and smell and sound—as if I'd drunk a healing potion, but for energy instead of health.

Only then did Teagan release me, and I stumbled back, gripping my wrist. A new spot of black ink was etched into my green skin: a black swirl no bigger than my fingernail. It itched like a new scab and I scratched at it furiously.

"Don't do that!" Teagan said, pulling my hand away. "The ink needs to settle, or the magic won't take."

Magic? I had *magic* now?

I looked up at the captain with wide eyes. "What kinda magic?"

"I've given you a Gain," Teagan replied. "You now have greater stamina to complete the tasks I have for you."

A Gain. Teagan had given me *a Gain!* I could hardly believe it! Wizards and mages used Gains to increase their strength and magic. If Teagan gave me one, it must've meant he had a *really* important job for me!

I looked up to see that the captain had returned to Lady Amaryl's side, lifting her hand to his lips.

"Thank you for your business," he said, removing his beautiful hat and bowing low.

"I expect a full account when you return," Lady Amaryl said, walking back up the dais to settle once again on her throne.

Everything was happening so fast—did I not even have time to get my things? I was grateful I'd at least strapped on my dagger last night. I'd have been sad to leave that behind.

I wondered if I would ever see the chateau or any of the other goblins again.

Captain Teagan was already heading for the door, and I hurried to follow him through the antechamber, down the great hall, and toward the chateau's entrance.

Two goblin guards pulled open the giant doors, and I took the first step of my new adventure and strode out into the sunlight.

Chapter Four

Frog-rot I hated sunlight. It hurt my eyes and made me sneeze, and I wished I could wear a hat like Teagan's for some shade.

We were barely out of the chateau when a figure suddenly appeared at our side. I jumped, but Teagan didn't even break stride.

"Took you long enough," said the new figure. He had a lilting accent, and when he pulled back his hood, I saw that he was an elf! His white hair was short, contrasting with his golden skin. "Have fun schmoozing the vampire queen?"

"Business as usual," was all Teagan said. "Let's go, Falaelor." Then he looked at me and added, "Keep up—it's a long walk to the docks."

It *was* a long walk—with the bright sun beating down on us. I had to look at the ground, relying on Teagan's feet to keep me going in the right direction.

Windtail tentatively stuck her head out from my vest, and part of me relaxed.

"Thanks for coming, Windtail!" I smiled. "It'd've been awfully lonely without you!"

The rat looked up at me with her wide, red eyes, nose twitching with worry.

"Don't be afraid!" I said cheerfully. "It's going to be an adventure!"

Even as I spoke, my chest bubbled with excitement. A special job with the captain I admired, the chance to work alongside my best friend, *and* getting a magic Gain, all in one day? I could hardly believe my luck!

Teagan and the elf walked side-by-side, talking in low voices about some place being "more shadowy." Whatever that meant. My stomach rumbled, and I pulled the sack of rotting fruits from my pocket, eating another piece.

Already, it felt like my new Gain was working, making it easier to keep pace with the human and elf. I wondered what I'd be doing that needed me to have a magic boost! Would we be battling pirates? Hunting for treasure? Rescuing a princess?

Still, Gain or not, I was completely out of breath by the time we reached the docks. The roar of the waves filled my ears before I saw them, and only then did I risk looking up, shading my eyes as I searched for Teagan's ship.

Instead, I saw the ocean, wide and shimmering green-blue. It was big and open and beautiful...and I knew straight away that I *did not like it.*

I froze, unable to look away from all that water. It was *so frog-rotting big*—much bigger than a swamp—and way too open. Where was anyone s'posed to hide? Where was the shade from the horrible sun?

My legs felt like they were stuck in quicksand. I couldn't do this. I didn't want to get on a ship after all—

Something grasped me by the back of my vest, and I was tugged forward, toward a small boat at the docks. I struggled frantically, trying to escape, but it was no use. Before I knew it, I was being pushed onto the boat. It rocked violently beneath my feet and I yelped, throwing myself onto the floor.

The elf laughed behind me, which was followed by a sigh from Teagan.

"*Please* try not to damage him, Falaelor," he said. "I'd hate for all that *schmoozing* to be for nothing."

The boat rocked again as Teagan and the elf climbed in after me, taking up their oars and starting to row. I didn't move—just sat stiffly at the bottom of the boat, unable to even lift my head for fear of that big water swallowing me whole.

Teagan and the elf didn't speak as they rowed, and time seemed to stretch on forever. How far away was the ship? Just how big was this awful water?

At last, they lifted their oars into the boat, and when I dared to sit up, I found myself face to face with the side of a ship.

"Come on," Teagan said, grabbing me by the arm and hoisting me to my feet. I wobbled as he pushed me toward the ship, but couldn't find any ladder—just a bunch of twisted ropes.

"B-but..." I stammered. "How do I—"

At that moment, something grabbed me again by the vest and hoisted me into the air. I screamed as wind whistled past my ears, but was just as quickly set down again on something solid. Chest heaving, I stumbled backwards into a wall and looked up to find—

"Jab!"

All my fears melted away as the enormous troll grinned down at me, and I bounced up and down.

"You were right, Jab! Teagan *did* hire me! I get to come with you on your adventure!"

Jab clapped, then leaned down, extending his fist. I pounded mine on top of it with new enthusiasm.

"What's this?" a new voice growled. "We wasted all this time for one, measly *goblin?*"

What a rude thing to say! I spun around to argue and almost yelped as a large orc stomped toward us. He had long tusks and a scar that ran down his left eye, which he fixed on me in a glower. I swallowed hard and ducked behind Jab.

"Watch your tone, Kurz." Teagan answered as he climbed onto the ship. "I got what I came for. Now gather the crew: I have an announcement to make."

Grumbling, the orc turned and began barking orders. "All hands on deck! Get your sorry tails up here!"

I looked up at Jab, who smiled and thumped me hard on the back. Soon the rest of the crew had gathered, standing at attention under Kurz's watchful eye. There were two more humans, two more orcs, and one giant troll with big blue eyes that matched his brother, Jab. I would have called out to greet Bash, but Teagan chose that very moment to speak.

"Crew, this is Falaelor." He gestured to the elf, who went to stand at his side. "While on this mission, you are to obey his orders as if they were coming from me. Is that understood?"

The crew gave their affirmative. I tried whispering the elf's name under my breath. "Fal— Fally— Falala—" I shook my head. Elves always had names that were too hard to pronounce. How was I supposed to remember a tongue twister like that?

"As of now," Teagan continued, "we make all possible speed toward Shadowmoor. There's a big score to be settled there, and I expect each and every one of you to give it your utmost."

A murmur went through the crew, and I looked up at Jab, who seemed just as confused as everyone else.

"Captain." The orc Kurz stepped forward and folded his arms. "What's this about? We just visited Shadowmoor a week ago."

Teagan clasped his hands behind his back. "That's none of your concern right now. All will be explained in time."

Kurz scowled. "Then what about him?" He gestured to me. "What's *he* got to do with anything?"

"Again," Teagan answered, "it's none of your concern. His job begins once we reach Shadowmoor, and until then you are to leave him alone." He fixed the orc with a glare. "No harm must come to him on this voyage. Is that understood?"

My chest warmed at the captain's words. He really cared about my safety, which was a nice change!

Kurz narrowed his eyes and turned his scary gaze on me. Was he mad at me for getting special treatment?

"Dismissed!" Teagan called.

With a huff, the orc began to move around, barking orders, and the crew jumped into action.

Jab patted my head with all the gentleness he could muster, then left to do some heavy work with Bash. I glanced around in time to watch as Captain Teagan and the elf disappeared into the main cabin.

And I was left standing alone in the middle of the ship. The crew moved quickly, so I backed myself into a corner, out of everyone's way. Cold, salty mist sprayed me. It wasn't the same as the home swamps, but the damp air felt homey and familiar.

Well, it looked like my adventure had finally begun, and I was *so* eager to see where it would lead! I may not've liked the ocean, but I was sure sailing was going to be frog-rotting fun!

Chapter Five

Sailing was *horrible*. As soon as we shipped out my stomach turned over, and I barely made it to the edge of the ship in time before losing my dinner.

"Ugh," I said, wiping my mouth on my sleeve.

Jab laughed and came to stand beside me. He was so tall, I worried he'd lose his balance and fall into the water. But I'd never seen Jab look so comfortable. He leaned out over the ship's edge, holding onto a rope that hung from above.

"I dunno how you stand it," I groused, clutching my stomach.

Jab just shrugged. Windtail had fled my shoulder, and sat perched on his instead, her nose pointed out toward the waves. *She* didn't seem bothered by this unstable deathtrap of a ship.

I breathed slowly through my mouth, trying to keep the sickness at bay. "What do you see in it?" I found myself asking. "I thought you'd prefer mountains!"

After a long moment, Jab leaned back into the ship. He raised his arms high above his head and fanned them out wide. He put a finger to his chest, then swept his arms out, gesturing to the water. He was smiling, a large, warm smile that crinkled his eyes, and he turned to me, tapping me twice on the top of my head.

I smiled despite myself. "Yeah," I said. "Alright. Ya got me there."

There *was* a kinda beauty to the ocean, no matter how much it made me want to curl up on the floor. "It reminds me of—"

My words died as the ship lurched, overturning my stomach, and I quickly aimed my head over the side.

But then the ship swayed more violently and I lost my footing, half-thrown over the side. Suddenly all I could see was water—so much water—an endless green consuming my vision and a roar of the waves that mixed with a voice in my ear.

'R.K. look out!'

Something clamped around my arm and I flew backwards, screaming as I was dropped onto the deck. My boots connected with solid planking, but my legs gave out, and I fell hard against a barrel.

I gasped and panted, feeling like my chest might explode. *I almost fell off the ship!*

Then Jab was right in front of me. His eyes were wide, mouth hanging open slightly, as if he were struggling to find words to speak. Then his expression changed, lips pinching together as he shook his head slowly, more solemn than I'd ever seen him before.

I shook my head in return, ears flapping. "No," I said, licking my lips. "I won't be doing that again. I'll make a mess on the deck and risk Kurz's wrath if I have to."

And I'd be staying as far away from the ship's edge as I possibly could.

Jab smiled a little at that and leaned away again. But a pinch in my leg made me jump, and I looked down to find Windtail digging her claws into my trousers, perched on her hind legs as she peered up at me.

'R.K.!' she squeaked. *'R.K., are you all right?'*

I blinked, vision swimming, sure I had misheard her. That couldn't have been what Windtail said, 'cause Windtail couldn't speak at all!

"Why're you talking?" I asked stupidly.

Windtail recoiled slightly, ducking her head and not meeting my gaze. Then she suddenly squeaked and dove into my trouser pocket, just before a loud thud made me jump.

I looked up and found the elf whats-his-name (Faerie Lord? Fallow Ore?) squatting on the deck, one hand stretched before himself in balance. Had he just...*jumped* from one of those pole things?

He lifted his eyes, which seemed to flicker like silver fire. Then he stood, poised and elegant as he strolled toward Jab and me. Jab quickly rose and dragged me to my feet. I stumbled and threw my arm over the barrel to keep myself upright. The elf stopped in front of me.

"You'd better watch yourself, goblin," he said, his voice quiet. "We wouldn't want you to tip over into the sea before your job was complete."

I trembled. Had the elf been *watching* us?

A shout rang through the air, and the door to the main cabin slammed open as Captain Teagan stormed out, Kurz close on his heels.

"So that's it?" the orc rumbled. "You expect us to just waltz up to the front door and attack without cause?"

"I expect you to do your job," Teagan answered calmly. "*You* work for *me*, and I expect you to keep the crew in line while Falaelor and I deal with the wizard."

Around us, other members of the crew began to duck out of sight, but I was rooted to the spot, gripped by the conversation.

"*The wizard*—bah!" Kurz spat over the side of the ship. "You mean that voided *Dark Lord* who rules over *Shadowmoor*? You can't be serious." He gestured with his head toward the elf—Faerie Lord. "You think you and that *shank* can take him down?"

"Silence!"

Teagan thrust out a hand, and I gasped. Did the captain really think he was strong enough to take on an orc?

But, to my surprise, Kurz just stood there, frozen, a ring of dark-light mist around his neck. The orc's hands scrambled frantically at his throat, but it was as if he were battling smoke. That's when I saw the dark mist extending like a thick rope, held tightly in Teagan's grip. The captain yanked on the rope, and Kurz fell to his hands and knees, head bowed as he choked and coughed.

"Do *not* forget," Teagan said, his voice deadly calm. "I am the one who brought you here, plucked from a cruel death at the hands of a Dark Lord. You owe me *everything*."

The captain took a step closer, and though his voice was a whisper, it seemed to ring loud and clear on the ship.

"The wizard lord of Shadowmoor is not the one you should fear. *I am*. You *will* obey, or you will find that dying for a Dark Lord would have been a much sweeter fate."

Silence hung in the air so long, I was almost too scared to breathe. Then, with a flick of his wrist, the dark-light disappeared from Teagan's grasp, leaving Kurz a sputtering mess on the deck.

With a sweep of his cloak and a flourish of his extraordinary hat, Teagan spun around, eyes searching until they fell on me. Frightened, I took a step closer to Jab. But the captain simply turned to Faerie Lord, who was leaning against the big pole.

"Come Falaelor," he said. "I require your assistance."

And with that, Teagan made his way back to the main cabin. The elf straightened and glanced back at me, smirking, before following the captain. I shivered and breathed a sigh of relief as soon as they were out of sight.

"You two!"

I squeaked as Kurz pushed himself to his feet, a hand over his throat as he struggled to draw a breath. He glared at me, then growled and turned to Jab.

"Get back to work!" he snarled, then winced and rubbed his neck. He looked over his shoulder to where Teagan and Faerie Lord had disappeared and sighed. "Void take them," he muttered. "They're going to get us all killed."

Then he stomped away without a backward glance.

A long moment passed—the deck so quiet, all I could hear was the splashing waves. Then I realized that Jab and me were the only two left standing on the deck.

I put a hand to the back of my neck, feeling the rise of the slave brand on my skin. Why was Teagan acting so mean? Sure, I didn't like Kurz, but I didn't not like him *that* much! I looked up at Jab.

"Is...is Captain Teagan usually like this?"

The troll didn't move for a long time. Then, slowly, he shook his head, brow furrowed.

My sleeve shifted, and I looked down as Windtail climbed up my arm to sit on my shoulder.

'I do not like the elf,' she whispered. *'There's something...off...about him.'*

I blinked at her a few times, trying to make sense of everything that was going on. Then I crossed my arms and glared at her.

"You've got some 'splaning to do."

*****

I squinted down at Windtail, who had the decency to look as sheepish as any rat could.

"You never told me you could talk!" I exclaimed. My head hurt and I was feeling pretty annoyed with everyone. Except maybe Jab.

The three of us were sitting in the cargo hold, away from the prying eyes of the Faerie Lord or Kurz or anyone else. Jab sat cross-legged on the floor as he sorted through his collection of rocks, arranging them in order to make a necklace. Windtail stood on his knee, wringing her paws.

'Well,' she said softly. *'I couldn't until quite recently.'*

It was so weird. Windtail didn't open her mouth, but I could hear her voice all the same. I pointed to her and looked at Jab. "You can hear her too, right?"

The troll looked up from his stones, first at the rat, then at me, and frowned as he shook his head.

"So I'm goin' crazy." That's all there was to it. I'd finally cracked. Barely a day on the ship and the sea air was already driving me insane.

'Well, no,' Windtail said. *'No one else can hear me 'cause you and I have a special bond.'*

"A bond?" My eyes went wide. "You mean...like a *magic* bond?"

The little rat put her paws on her hips. *'Well how else do you think I'm able to talk to you?'*

"Whoa." This was all so sudden. I rubbed my scalp in thought. "But like...what kind of a magic bond is it?"

Windtail thought about it for a moment, nose twitching.

"I don't exactly know how it works," she said at last, *'but I think it's like your bond with Teagan. It got stronger after he gave you the Gain, and that's when I realized I could talk.'*

Jab gave a little grunt, his stones making a steady *clack clack* noise as he sorted through them.

"Sorry you can't hear her, Jab," I said.

The troll shrugged in dismissal. He held a large needle to the blue dragon-y stone and worked on carving out a hole. I sat down cross-legged beside him.

"Jab," I said, "do you like working here? For Teagan, I mean?"

Of course Jab had told me all about his different adventures while working in Teagan's crew, and he'd seemed to like it when he told me. But something about the way Captain Teagan had punished Kurz...well, it made me nervous.

Jab nodded his head. Then he shook it. Then he paused, lifted his hand, and tilted it from side to side.

"So, sometimes you like it," I guessed, "and sometimes you don't?"

Jab nodded, then smiled and pointed at me. I couldn't help but smile back.

"I like being here with you too." I may not have liked the ocean, but I liked hanging out with my friend.

I suppressed a yawn. It'd been a long night and day, but I was looking forward to tomorrow. Surely this adventure could only go up from here!

Chapter Six

I stared in disgust at the sewage outfall sticking out of the cliffside. As if this adventure could get *any worse*. The waters in this region already smelled bad—I couldn't imagine how bad it would smell *inside* the sewers. I was grateful we wouldn't be—

"The goblin and I will be taking the sewers," Captain Teagan announced as he addressed the crew. I slumped, and Jab chuckled, thumping me on the back. "Falaelor will be taking the tower, and the rest of you will be attacking the main gate."

Kurz scowled at the human. "And how do you expect us to take the castle, *captain?*"

Teagan looked at Kurz and, for a horrible moment, I thought he might summon another dark-light attack.

"I don't expect you to take the castle," he finally answered. "Your job is simply to provide a distraction. Falaelor will handle the guards and clear the path for you."

I peered up at Jab, who looked just as surprised as I felt. He and Bash were readying the little boat, but they kept glancing at Teagan and me.

Everyone kept glancing at Teagan and me. It'd taken us three days to reach the island, and by now the whole crew was on edge. This More Shadowy place was really living up to its name. Dark smoke shrouded the land, as if a giant storm cloud had settled on top of it. Supposedly, there was a civilized harbor for docking on the far side of the island, but *noooo*. Captain Teagan just *had* to take the most distressing route of all—and had to take *me* with him.

Teagan turned toward the Faerie Lord. "Your contact had better come through."

"Oh, don't you worry," the elf replied. "Everything has been planned out."

Teagan nodded. "Good. Then I'll see you on the other side." And with that, he climbed into the little boat. "Let's go, goblin."

Desperate, I looked up once more at Jab and held up my fist. "I'll try and find you as soon as we're through!"

The mountain troll didn't hesitate to tap his fist against mine.

Stomach in knots, I clambered into the boat, gripping the edges for dear life as Jab and Bash slowly lowered it into the water with a *thunk* that nearly sent me tumbling overboard. I tried not to panic as Teagan took up the oars and started rowing toward the outfall.

Sadly, I watched as the ship was slowly consumed by the dark mist.

The silence was almost as bad as the smell. Captain Teagan kept his eyes fixed straight over my head, so that the swish of the oars and the splash of the waves were all I had for company. I refused to let go of the boat's edges, afraid of upsetting the balance, so I couldn't tell how far we still needed to go until the boat actually bumped the side of the cliff face.

Teagan stood and threw a rope over a jagged rock, anchoring the boat in place. We were right up next to the outfall, which was little more than a tunnel carved into the cliffside. Long metal bars stretched from top to bottom of its wide mouth.

"Uh, *that's* the entrance?" I said, looking from the tunnel, to Teagan, then back at the tunnel again. "How're we s'posed to get through?"

In answer, Teagan pulled us closer to the outfall, then reached up and began tapping on the bars. After a few, his tap made a scraping noise, and he paused. Gripping the bar with his hand, he gave it a tug and, with a loud *screech*, it came free.

"Good," he said, tossing the bar into the water. "Falaelor delivered as promised."

The gap in the bars was just wide enough to squeeze through. And without so much as a warning, Teagan grabbed my arm and hoisted me up onto the stone. I let out a squeal of fright, scrambling to grip the bars and not fall backwards.

"In!" Teagan commanded. "We don't have time to waste!"

I hesitated, not wanting to be anywhere near that awful smell. But what else could I do? Gritting my teeth, I used the bars to pull myself into the tunnel beyond.

Fighting back a retch, I buried my nose in my arm and looked around, my eyes adjusting easily to the darkness. The tunnel stretched as far as I could see, and though it was quite spacious, I hunkered down, fearful of some monster appearing out of the shadows. A steady stream of muck lurked on the tunnel floor, flowing through the outfall. I was grateful to be wearing boots.

Another splash made me jump, and I looked around to find Captain Teagan right behind me. He held up a lantern and was checking something in his hand. A pocketwatch? He had to bend almost in half just to stand in the tunnel and I might've laughed at the sight if I hadn't been fighting for my life against the stench.

"Let's go," Teagan said, pushing past me to walk in front.

I blinked, wishing he'd put out the light. But I knew how frail human eyesight was, so I kept my mouth shut.

We walked a long while, fighting against the flow of the sewer water. Teagan's lantern cast a dull light on the walls, and it took a long time for my eyes to adjust and take in our surroundings. The tunnels were made of a curved stone, darkened and fouled by the sewage. Then the light began to bend as we reached a fork in the tunnels, going in opposite directions. I wrung my hands nervously, wondering how Teagan could possibly figure out where to go.

He glanced right, then left, shining his lantern both ways. Then he lifted his free hand, fingers curling inward, and I jumped as a ball of his dark-light magic crackled to life.

Teagan held up his hand, and when he turned to the left, the ball of dark-light began to sputter.

"Don't lag behind," he hissed, voice echoing off the walls as he stepped into the tunnel. I shivered and hurried to follow.

The smell was almost suffocating, and I held my vest over my nose. Somehow though, Captain Teagan didn't seem bothered by it. His clothes remained pristine, his wonderful hat still perched on his head (though the feathers did look a bit droopy).

Teagan kept up a brisk pace, following wherever the dark-light moved. But I, for one, was completely lost. The tunnels made so many turns and the outfall was so far behind us that I doubted I'd be able to find my way out again. Just how far *did* these tunnels go? We truly seemed like rats in a maze. Except for Windtail, who really *was*.

Everything sounded strange too, with even the smallest noise vibrating across the stone walls, so that every drip of murky water sounded like a drum. That, combined with the vile smell, was starting to make my head hurt.

It was, in every way possible, utterly miserable. My one comfort was Windtail, still curled in my pocket. Though she didn't speak, I could still feel her discomfort.

The light bent again as we passed another fork in the tunnels, and something shifted in the shadows. Teagan swung toward it, thrusting out his lantern and casting the light on—

A rat! A fat, gray thing, perched on its hind legs and blinking against the brightness.

What luck! I grinned and squatted down, hand extended as I made clicking sounds with my tongue.

"Don't do that!" Teagan hissed, sweeping his cloak and startling me so that I almost fell back into the muck. "I don't want that vermin anywhere near me!"

I sniffed in contempt and immediately regretted it as I took the full brunt of the sewer stench. I glared at Teagan. Rats weren't vermin! They were scavengers, spies, resilient creatures, and excellent friends! Why, sometimes rats were even nicer than humans!

But Teagan took no notice of me. He scowled at the rat, then turned and continued his march through the darkness.

"Come, goblin," he said.

I balled my hands into fists. "Rat King."

Teagan froze and looked back over his shoulder, a strange expression on his face. "What did you say?"

I took a deep breath through my mouth and drew myself up to my full height. "My name is Rat King."

Teagan raised one eyebrow, then looked me up and down.

"Yes," he said, turning around again. "I suppose you are." He glanced at his pocketwatch. "Now get moving."

My shoulders slumped. He could have at least *acted* like he cared.

After a few paces I heard a tiny patter, and when I looked over my shoulder, I saw the rat following at a distance, eyes reflecting Teagan's lamplight.

It tilted its head up at me, steps hesitant at first, then growing more eager. It expertly avoided the muck at our feet, and I smiled to myself. Teagan didn't know what he was talking about. Rats were smart creatures. They knew how to navigate these tunnels better than we did!

We walked on and, as we went, I heard more tiny patters as even more rats joined the first. They kept to the shadows, avoiding Teagan's light, and I was comforted by their presence, knowing I wasn't alone.

I was used to working at night with little contact from the sun, so the dark didn't usually bother me. But down in these sewers, there was no way to tell how much time was passing, and it made me nervous. I wished I could've looked at Teagan's pocketwatch. Had it been minutes since we first entered? Hours? My thoughts turned to Jab and Bash, and even Kurz. Had they reached the harbor yet? Had they started their attack? I hoped not—I didn't want them to fall into danger.

My stomach rumbled in spite of the smelly circumstances, and I wondered how much longer this would take. There was still one last piece of rotten fruit in my pocket, but I dared not open the bag and risk spoiling it in this foul place!

RAT KING

At long last, Teagan stopped, and I peered around him, shocked to find that we had reached three paths, all of them barred. How were we supposed to go forward now?

The captain did a slow turn, lifting the dark-light, and stopped when the magic began to crackle again, pointing toward the left-side tunnel. He held his lantern closer, pushing it through the bars, but even then it was impossible to see the end of the tunnel.

Teagan closed his hand, putting out the dark-light. Then he abruptly swiveled back toward me and I jumped, falling back a step.

"Alright, goblin," he said. "This is where your services come in." He gestured with his head. "Squeeze through those bars and follow the tunnel as far as it will go. It will lead you straight to the waste chute. You'll find a lever in the wall." Teagan fixed me with a hard glare. "You will need to pull the lever *down*."

I gazed into the barred-off tunnel, stomach twisted into knots. "Right. And then what?"

"And then nothing. The lever will lift the bars for me, so you can wait for me there."

I frowned. "But what'll I need to do then?"

Teagan scowled. "Nothing! You'll wait for further instructions!"

I wrinkled my nose. "But is...is that it? The whole reason you hired me from Lady Amaryl was to *flip a switch?*"

"Did you want something more *difficult?*" Teagan said the last bit with a sneer. But the truth was...*yeah*. I *had* been hoping for more of a challenge—something interesting and adventurous, something worthy of wearing a big, phenomenal hat like his!

Flipping a switch...that was just more *grunt work.*

Suppressing a huff, I ambled over to the entrance. The bars were pretty close together, but if I gripped one and turned sideways, I was just able to squeeze between them. It was tight—I had to suck in and flatten my ears—but I managed to pass through and let out a heavy sigh, leaning my hands on my knees.

"Well, get on with it!" Teagan barked. "We haven't got all day!"

I turned back and glared at him, but I knew he was right. Jab was still out there, in danger, and we needed to hurry to meet the crew.

Taking a deep breath, I ran deeper into the tunnel. It was dark, but my eyes appreciated it more as the harsh lamplight faded from view. After awhile, I noticed the *splash splash* of murky waters changed to the *clomp clomp* of my boots on dry stone. This tunnel sounded like it hadn't been used in awhile.

I panted as I ran and quickly slowed to a trot once I was out of Teagan's sight. *Frog-rot*, I was *really* out of shape. I'd have to fix that once this adventure was over.

Adventure—bah! What a joke! *This* certainly wasn't the kind of adventure I'd hoped for. Treasure hunts and daring battles and exciting discoveries—weren't *those* supposed to be what adventures were all about? Not sneaking through sewers and *pulling levers*.

"What do you think we'll find in this Dark Lord's castle?" I whispered.

Windtail climbed out of my pocket and onto my shoulder. *'A Dark Lord, I s'pose,'* she said, unhelpfully.

We finally reached the end of the tunnel and, just as Teagan had said, there was a hatch with a lever next to it, pushed upright.

'Do we have *to do this?'* Windtail said. *'I have a bad feeling.'*

"It's probably the smell." I put my hands on my hips. She was right though: I didn't like anything about this mission. "We *gotta*," I said. "We gotta help Jab, and this is the only way into the castle!"

'So Teagan says!' Windtail wrinkled her nose. *'Yet he throws all his crew at the front gate, then skulks down here in the shadows! I don't like it.'*

I sighed. "Me neither." Yet I still reached up and took hold of the lever mounted on the wall. It was heavy, and my arms strained as I tried to pull it down.

"Goblin!" Teagan's voice echoed in the distance. "What's taking so long?"

I ground my teeth. "Workin' on it!" I shouted back. Then I jumped up and pulled with all my might. The lever creaked and the hatch made a scraping sound.

'That's it!' Windtail encouraged. *'Put your back into it!'*

"It's hard enough putting my front into it!" I jumped again and tugged down, repeating the process over and over. The scraping sound grew louder yet, for all my struggles, I couldn't get the frog-rotting thing to come down!

"Stupid tall folk!" I growled, swinging a leg up and pulling myself over until I was sitting on the lever. "Never accounting for us little guys who don't got the strength for this kinda work!"

"Goblin!" Teagan yelled again.

Ignoring him, I pushed myself up until I was standing on the lever, boots together as I fought for balance. Then I jumped as high as I could and landed with a *clank*. The hatch jerked up briefly and released a burst of murky water.

"Uh oh," I said, then cupped my hands over my mouth and shouted, "Incoming!"

With everything I had, I gave one great leap, bringing the lever down with a loud *snap!*

I fell onto the ground and just managed to flatten myself against a wall as the hatch sprung open and vomited a torrent of sludge. It slithered down the tunnel, releasing a newfound stench that made me gag. I buried my nose in my sleeve, taking shallow breaths.

Moments later, splashing footsteps signaled Teagan's approach, and I managed to straighten myself up to my full height just as the captain came into view.

"That took longer than expected," he groused.

I glared. Not even a 'thank you' for my troubles? I was gonna make some serious complaints about this workforce environment when everything was over!

Teagan examined the open hatch, muttering under his breath as he looked up the chute. He paused for a moment, then looked back at me.

"Good work with this!" he said. "Could you come over here? I've got more for you to do, after all."

I perked up. "Really?" Maybe I'd been too hasty.

Teagan nodded and pointed at the hatch. "Think you could climb up this chute and scout the area for me?"

I grinned. A scouting mission! Now *that* was more like the adventure I was looking for!

Hurrying over, I tilted my head to look up the chute. It was narrow, but not uncomfortably so, and far up in the distance I could see a pinprick of light. A strange shimmer hung in the air before it, reflecting Teagan's lantern light. It was kinda pretty in the darkness.

I glanced once more at Teagan, who nodded encouragingly. Then, eagerly, I hoisted myself up inside.

'Wait R.K.—!'

Something exploded, and blinding pain shot down my body, like a lightning strike. Hot and cold scorched over my skin, sizzling in my ears and teeth. For a long moment, all I could do was stand there in unending, blinding agony.

The next thing I knew, I was on the ground, twitching. I managed to crack an eye open and saw a large boot pass above my face as Teagan stepped over me.

"Good work, goblin," he said pleasantly. "You did beautifully. But now your services are no longer required."

Like a worm shriveling in the sun, I felt the slave brand on my neck dry up and fade from my skin. And the last thing I saw was Teagan disappearing into the chute—plunging me into darkness.

Chapter Seven

The cold stone dug into my back as I lay there. My body screamed as I writhed in the most excruciating pain of my life. But even that couldn't compare to the drowning feeling in my chest as the magic of my Gain slowly started to drain away.

No, no, no!

I twisted my hand and watched in despair as the inky brand on my wrist shrank away, till it was no bigger than a pinprick. Then, like a knife cutting into my chest, I felt my connection to the magic snap.

And just like that, I was a grunt again, one hit away from death.

'R.K.? R.K. wake up!'

With a great effort, I managed to turn my head and found Windtail's face close to mine.

'Wake up!'

"Mmm'wake," I croaked, wincing as the words pierced my skull.

'You can't just stay here, R.K. You need to get up!'

Blinking seemed to be the only thing I was good at right now, and even that felt exhausting. I closed my eyes again, shutting everything else out and letting the darkness wash over me. The pain had faded a little, but it still ached in my bones and itched on my skin, and all I wanted to do was lie here forever.

Something sharp pinched my shoulder, and I startled. "Wha—? Wha's'goin'on?" My tongue felt like it was coated with mud.

Windtail chittered angrily. *'I think there was some kind of magic in the chute. When you tried to climb up, it blasted you.'*

My head pounded like a war drum. Windtail's words weren't sticking to my brain, so I closed my eyes again. "What're...you talkin'..." I couldn't find the words to say, but somehow Windtail seemed to understand.

'Teagan used you to destroy the magic barrier.'

"Teagan..." I repeated. "S'good guy..."

'No R.K.,' Windtail said. *'Teagan left you! He used you, then he left you down here to die!'*

What? No, that couldn't be right! Teagan was a good captain...wasn't he?

'R.K. listen, you have to get up. We have to go rescue Jab!'

My eyes flew open.

"Jab...?" I croaked. "What—"

'He's been captured.'

"Captured?" It took all my strength just to push myself up onto one elbow and, when I did, I had to blink several times at the little white rat in front of me. She kept duplicating, until there were more rats than I could count. "There're so many of you...." I mumbled.

'No,' Windtail said, *'there are many of us.'* She glanced around as more rats pressed closer. *'They told me these sewers expand through the entire island, and there are many rats that live in them. They saw Jab and the rest of the crew get captured.'*

"Jab..." I muttered again. If he's been captured, that meant I hadn't been fast enough to help him. I'd failed. But if he was still alive....

Windtail stood in front of me, nose twitching in worry as I struggled to push myself up. Everything hurt, and I felt heavy, as if a sack of rocks had been tied to my back. The tunnel swam around me, and I almost fell back onto my face.

But something held me up, and a loud chittering filled my ears as several sharp prickles dug into my arm. I lifted my head and was surprised to find the rats by my side, holding me up.

The sight of so many new friends trying to help filled me with a new strength, and I dragged myself up and onto my knees. My head felt a bit clearer now, and I counted at least a dozen rats, plus Windtail, staring up at me.

"Thank you," I said, wincing as I put a hand to my chest. The sudden absence of magic left me feeling empty and cold. I...I'd just have to find more somehow. I *would* get more magic, if only to be rid of this hollow ache.

I looked back over my shoulder and saw that the hatch was shut. "No escaping that way." I needed to rescue Jab, but how was I ever gonna find my way out of this horrible place? Without Teagan's magic to guide me, I was completely lost.

I wrinkled my nose. *Teagan!* I'd been so excited to join his crew, and what had he done? Hurt me and my friends, bossed me and everyone else around, and now he'd used me and left me for dead! I balled my hands into fists, deciding then and there that I hated Teagan and his stupid hat!

For a few seconds, I stewed in my anger. Then I sighed and shook my head. No, I could never hate that incredible hat.

Besides, now was not the time for revenge. I needed to find Jab and break him out before anything else happened to him. I might hate Teagan, but I didn't hate his crew, and right now they needed my help.

Desperately, I looked at all the rats sitting before me. I had no one else, nothing left, except for these scavengers, spies, and resilient creatures who'd done their best to help me.

"Please," I said. "Do you know the way into the castle?"

The rats turned to one another, chittering among themselves. And it was...strange. I'd always felt a kinship to rats...it's why I'd chosen my name. But for the first time in my life, I felt I could almost *understand* them.

A fat gray rat stepped forward with a squeak, and Windtail turned back to me.

'They do!' she said excitedly.

Panting, I hauled myself to my feet, wincing as a new pain throbbed in one of my legs. Windtail bounded up to perch on my shoulder.

"Can you take me there?" I asked.

Immediately, one by one, the rats turned and ran down the tunnel. Drawing my dagger, I limped after them, quick as I could. The entrance bars had fallen again, but it was still easy to squeeze through, and soon I was following the rats into the next tunnel. It was much easier now without the lantern light, and I kept a close watch on the rats as they ran.

We wound through many twists and turns, more slowly than before as I struggled with the pain in my leg. The rats measured their pace, darting back and forth to make sure I was keeping stride. But the pain was not unbearable. In fact, it only seemed to urge me onward. I picked up the pace and, though it hurt, soon I was running with renewed strength.

More rats appeared out of the shadows, joining us. Windtail was right: there were so many of them down here: a whole rat kingdom—fit for a king.

And then, just as suddenly as we had begun, the rats stopped, and I skidded to a halt.

There was a door. An *actual* door, large and imposing, made of an impressive dark wood that was intricately carved. It looked like something that belonged in a chapel—not buried here in the sewers.

"This?" I said, marveling at the craftsmanship. "*This* is the way into the castle?"

Several of the rats scampered around, chittering among themselves, and I could practically feel the confusion radiating off of them.

"What's wrong?" I asked Windtail, and she hopped down and began to talk with the others. After a moment she turned back to me.

'It's all so confusing....' she said. *'These rats swear they were taking you to the dungeons, but they don't recognize this door!'*

Looking the door up and down, I was startled to realize that the ceiling was much higher now, more easily accessible for humans.

I laughed in spite of myself. Had Teagan known about this entrance? Surely he would've preferred such an impressive door instead of that dirty old chute!

I stepped up and tried the handle, though of course it'd be locked—

The door clicked and swung inward without so much as a creak, and I jumped back with a yelp.

The other side led to somewhere *really* fancy, with plush red carpet and gold on the pretty corner parts of the ceiling. A hallway stretched before us, the walls a dark, polished stone, lit with torches.

'This doesn't look like a dungeon....' Windtail whispered.

"No," I said, pressing a hand against the door frame. "This has to be the castle." It reminded me of Lady Amaryl's chateau: the vampire queen craved the finer things in life, and this was *so* much finer than what she had.

I wiggled my nose. The air smelled better here too, and I was eager to leave the foul sewers behind. I took a step forward—

'Don't!' Windtail's voice was shrill as she scampered around my feet. *'Don't you remember what happened last time we tried some random door?'*

"Uhhh...right," I mumbled. I moved from one side of the door to the other, twisting and turning as I searched for a shimmer, or whatever it was I'd seen in the chute. But I couldn't find one. No shimmer, no weird aura, nothing. I took a tentative step closer, and the rats crowded around.

A thought popped into my head: *send one of the rats through first,* and I balked. What? No way! That's something *Teagan* had done, and I wasn't gonna be like him. What kinda horrible boss sent his henchman in to do the dirty work? My ears flapped as I shook my head in disgust.

I edged closer, boots scraping over stone. No, I had to try it myself.

"Stand back," I told them, taking a deep breath and stepping forward until my nose was a hair's breadth from the threshold.

Tentatively, I reached out a hand, one finger extended, and poked it through.

Nothing happened.

Carefully, I extended my entire hand over the threshold.

No reaction.

I took a deep breath, chest pounding, and crept forward, thrusting my whole arm through.

There was a surprising lack of pain.

"*Frog-rot!*" I yelled, and jumped all the way through the door.

I held my breath, waiting to see if anything would come at me: spike in the walls, a trap door beneath my feet, some kinda horrible lightning magic. But nothing happened. And the longer I stood there, the more my shoulders eased until, finally, I released my breath.

It was just an ordinary door. A magnificently *fancy* ordinary door, leading to a majestically fancier hallway. I took a long deep breath through my nose.

"Huh."

'What is it?' Windtail asked.

"Well it's just…it definitely doesn't smell like a dungeon."

'You're right,' Windtail said, creeping forward. Several of the rats followed, chittering. *'Oh dear,'* she added.

"What?"

'Now our friends are saying this is the third story of the castle!'

My eyebrows shot up. "But…surely we haven't climbed up all that way to get here? We didn't even use any stairs!"

I took a few steps down the hallway. The other rats were darting to and fro around my feet, and Windtail scrambled up to sit on my shoulder.

'I really don't like this, R.K.,' she said, digging her claws into my shoulder.

"Well," I sighed, "at least we made it into the castle, and that's what matters. We just need to find a different way to the dungeons and—"

But the words stuck in my throat, and all the air was sucked from my lungs. Something...*heavy* tugged in my chest, as if a rope had been tied beneath my ribcage, squeezing so hard I couldn't breathe.

Magic.

My feet stumbled forward of their own accord. I *had* to walk. I *had* to move in the direction that rope was pulling me.

'R.K.? Where are you going?'

I was vaguely aware of Windtail's voice in my ear, but it was like listening through water. I couldn't answer—all I could do was walk, steps silent over the plush carpet. The hall seemed to stretch forever. When it split in two, the tug pulled me right, then left, then right again. I passed door after door. Why was the castle so big? And where were all the people? Each step led me deeper, yet there were no signs of life. It was creepy.

I walked until my feet found a flight of stairs, and I could feel the tug pulling me upward. Slowly, agonizingly, I had to follow.

'R.K. What are you doing?' Windtail cried. *'We're supposed to be rescuing Jab in the dungeons!'*

Jab. I needed to rescue Jab! I'd promised to help him. I needed to go to the dungeons....

But I couldn't stop my ascent. I climbed, step by step, as if stuck in a nightmare.

'R.K....talk to me!'

But I couldn't.

The climb was slow and made my legs ache as I limped. But the higher I climbed, the more the weight in my chest eased, and I couldn't stop myself. I couldn't *not* keep going up.

I started to run, pushing through the burning in my legs and the ache in my lungs. Higher and higher, round and round as the staircase began to wind. I couldn't breathe. I couldn't stop. I was dying. I'd drop dead from exhaustion—

And then there was a door.

I stopped.

It was large and imposing, with a fashionable brass knocker, as if somebody'd be waiting on the other side to offer me a cup of tea.

The source of the tug came from somewhere beyond it.

I walked slowly forward, trying with every step to turn away, to make myself go back and find Jab. But this force, this *magic*, kept me stuck here.

A wail escaped my throat and I gripped my head. I had to go in. I didn't want to, but the tug was so strong it felt like it would rip my heart right out of my chest and—

'R.K.! Snap out of it!'

I gasped and looked down to find Windtail, staring anxiously up at me. The other rats from the sewers were still with me as well, tails twitching with agitation.

"I'm sorry," I said. "I don't know why—I gotta—"

'Just do it,' Windtail said gently. *'See what's on the other side. Then we can get out of here.'*

Nodding, I took a running leap and grasped the knocker with both hands. I felt magic burst forth from the door, and it swung outward.

Sound exploded in my ears. Lightning crackled in the air. And directly in front of me stood Captain Teagan.

His back to me, Teagan's arms were sprawled, as if to catch the lightning with his bare hands. Or was he *making* the lightning? It was hard to tell. What I *could* tell was that on the other end of the lightning was another person.

The wizard!

He stood on the far side of the room, blood red cloak billowing behind him as he extended his hands, pushing back against the lightning. But even as I watched, he lifted one hand away and, with a flick of his wrist, summoned a ball of fire in his palm.

But instead of throwing it at Teagan, he threw it to the side. Following the arch, I gasped when I saw that it was aimed at none other than Faerie Lord! The elf held a glowing sword in one hand, which he swung wildly at the wizard. But with a quick step, the wizard ducked out of the way, keeping contact with the lighting at his fingertips. It was kinda impressive.

Faerie Lord swung around for another attack, and Teagan edged his way forward. He shouted something, and the wizard shouted back, but I couldn't hear a frog-rotting thing over all the noise.

Besides, I had more important things to deal with: like trying to escape. This was a game of wizards and heroes, and I was just a rat caught in the middle.

Turning on my heel, I tried to run—only to find the door shut and bolted behind me. I banged my fists against it, searching for another knocker. But there was nothing.

I was trapped.

Spinning around, I flattened my back against the door, looking around wildly for any means of escape. Close at my heels, the rats had grown frantic. They crawled up my legs and all over my chest, searching for a place to hide.

Teagan and Faerie Lord fought with a speed and agility I'd never seen before. With Teagan's magic and Faerie Lord's strength, they made a formidable force. Yet for all their efforts, they couldn't land one hit on the wizard. He grinned as he fought, casting fireballs at Faerie Lord, while still holding back Teagan's lightning. It was like a dangerous and brightly lit dance that all three of them worked hard to maintain.

"Wow," I whispered. That wizard was *really* impressive.

The wizard startled as if he heard me, and locked eyes with mine. His face scrunched up in confusion, head tilting slightly to the side, and for a brief moment I couldn't look away, captured in a gaze that seemed to span decades. No, *centuries*—a flood of wisdom and anger and pain stemming from hundreds of years of survival against all odds—

A glowing sword suddenly sprouted from the wizard's chest.

The lightning died, and for a moment a deafening silence rang in my ears, almost more terrible than the noise.

The wizard slumped forward, and Faerie Lord straightened up behind him. Swiftly, he withdrew the sword, and I was surprised to see no traces of blood—just the wizard holding the place where the sword had been, his expression full of shock as he fell to his knees.

Then Teagan was whooping, and I jumped in surprise.

"No..." I whispered, disappointment flooding my chest.

Teagan laughed loudly and swaggered forward. "Not so powerful after all, eh, Varyon?" He shoved a hand into the wizard's cloak. The wizard tried to resist, but Faerie Lord came up behind and wrapped an arm around his neck. When Teagan finally stepped away, he lifted his hand, and I saw that he held some kind of strange glimmering gemstone. It was smooth and round and glowing red from within.

And in that moment, time seemed to slow, until Teagan, Faerie Lord, and the wizard were all frozen in place.

I gasped and stumbled forward as, once again, a deafening silence attacked my ears. Color drained from the world until all that was left was gray—gray and the red shining from the stone in Teagan's hand.

The stone began to glow, brighter and brighter, until it filled the world with red, and I had to throw my arm up over my eyes to shield them from the piercing light.

And then, like a thousand voices speaking at once, words broke through the silence.

"A shadow walks where light once lay
The path grows dark each passing day
Unless the light itself can hold
The heart shall burn with dark untold"

"Uhhhhh..." I winced as the voices rose in pitch and volume. "I don't understand!"

Yet the voices carried on, ignoring me, even though I was *sure* they were talking *to* me. Which I thought was pretty rude.

"Through endless power will fate be sealed
What once was hid shall be revealed
Unless this curse the heart can break
The dark that slept shall soon awake."

"Alriiiiight," I said. "That's, uh, that's very informative! Thanks!"

And then, with a sound like shattering glass, the red light exploded around me. The frozen gray moment was over, and time resumed. Only then did I realize I was standing next to

Teagan, though I had no memory of walking forward. Teagan himself startled as he caught sight of me.

"What in the Void?" he gasped. "How did you get here?"

Then everything happened at once.

A fireball burst from the wizard's hands and hit Teagan square in the chest. Teagan stumbled backwards, the stone flying from his grasp.

Faerie Lord leapt forward and caught it out of the air and, with a roundhouse kick, slammed his boot into Teagan's side.

Teagan cried out and fell back against a window with a loud crash, and I watched in horror as the captain disappeared over the edge.

A noise drew my attention back, and I found Faerie Lord laughing as he held the stone up in triumph. Then he turned toward me, head tilted as if he'd only just noticed I was there. He grinned widely and, before I could even blink, he was in front of me.

"Thanks for the help," he said. Then his boot connected with my mouth and sent me flying back against the door.

'R.K.!'

Windtail's voice was in my head, but I couldn't see her. I slumped against the door, unable to move, unable to breathe. I tasted copper as green blood dripped from my mouth. He'd probably knocked out a tooth, as well. That'd be annoying.

I felt my last drop of stamina drain away, but all I could think about was Jab still stuck in the dungeons. If only I'd tried harder!

I closed my eyes, and there was a bright light behind them. Oh, everyone was right! You *did* see a light before you died! I just hoped it wasn't that mean old sun again....

Something gripped my arm and I gasped, the air ragged in my chest. I opened my eyes and found myself face to face with the wizard. He sprawled on the floor before me, wheezing as he struggled to keep his head upright. This close, I could see that he was an elf, his gray skin going pale, his red eyes burning like hot embers as they glared at me.

"I will *not* let you escape so easily," the elf snarled. "You cost me *everything*, so now this all will cost *you!*"

I shuddered under the weight of his gaze, but the wizard kept a hold on my arm, like an iron vice, as if he could snatch me away from death by sheer force of will.

Then I felt a burst of power unlike anything I'd ever experienced before.

It was piercing light and dulling dark and fire in my veins and ice on my skin and I screamed and screamed as the magic raked through my chest, scraping out my insides and replacing every part of me with something larger, darker, *terrible, painful.* It was too much, and I was going to explode from the inside out. I was burning. I was drowning. My chest was expanding.

"You will heed my words and rule until I return!" said the wizard. "Don't let the steward try and take control!" His grip tightened. "Do not let him near my research! The fate of this world—and the next—depends upon it!"

I blinked, those fiery red eyes filling all of my vision.

And then they vanished in a puff of black smoke.

Darkness swirled around me, as if all the light had been ripped out of the room, leaving only a gaping void in its wake.

The pain was gone.

I was on my feet.

And oh...*I had magic again.*

Chapter Eight

The magic flowed through my veins, vast and powerful, and everything burned with a strange new clarity. Brighter, but it didn't irritate my eyes. Louder, but it didn't hurt my ears. I had so much I felt I might burst.

'R.K.?'

I blinked, turning slowly to look down at Windtail. Had she shrunk? Or had I grown? No, it must have been a trick of the light, because she scampered up my leg to rest on my shoulder as usual.

'Your eyes,' she said.

"What about them?"

'They're...glowing.'

Huh. Maybe that explained why they felt so dry? I shrugged. "I feel normal."

No. I felt *incredible*.

A thrill went through my chest, and I felt like I could do *anything*.

I noticed then that I was holding...what was this, jewelry? I held up what appeared to be a gold medallion encrusted with a bright, shining ruby. It was pretty, but I found myself wrinkling my nose. What was with this guy and the color red?

'What's that?' Windtail asked.

"No idea, but I think it belonged to the wizard."

I pulled the chain over my neck and tucked the medallion beneath my shirt. As I did, I noticed a spot of ink on my skin, and with new excitement, pulled back my sleeve and found a new magical brand on my wrist. Only this was a *lot* bigger than the one Teagan had given me. This time, the brand covered my entire wrist and crept up my forearm, swirling black over green, creating a weird, repetitive pattern I'd never seen the likes of before.

Fractals.

The word came to me so abruptly that I jumped, whirling around to see if someone had walked into the room. But no, it was just me and the rats. Strange...I didn't think I'd ever heard that word before, but I instantly knew it's what the pattern was called. How neat!

I looked around the room, able to appreciate it now that there wasn't a crazy battle going on. It was...kinda boring actually. Just a library, with more books than seemed reasonable. The only interesting part was the stained glass windows, though one of them lay in fragments on the floor. The one Teagan had fallen through.

My eyes widened. No...it couldn't be!

I ran forward and, gingerly, lifted Teagan's hat from where it had fallen. All the phoenix feathers were gone and it was frayed and burned around the rim. But it was still *magnificent*. And now, it was *mine*.

Grinning, I placed the hat on my head, a fitting crown for a king.

I did a little jig.

'But what do we do now?' Windtail's voice cut through my reverie.

What *were* we going to do? What did *I* want to do? It seemed that there were endless possibilities spread out before me. Now, I could practically feel the magic thrumming in my chest, like a great bubble full of energy. And I knew if I wanted to, I could use that magic to do whatever I wanted.

I just needed to figure out how to use it first.

"Well," I said, running my fingers along the brim of my new hat. "I suppose the only thing we can do: we gotta rescue Jab!"

'But how are we going to do that?'

I grinned. "Isn't it obvious? I'll ask all my friends!"

I turned back to face the room. The library was in shambles, books and papers strewn across the floor.

My research.

Huh. Obviously not *my* research since I'd never been here before in my life, but it seemed important anyhow. I stepped to the door, and this time it opened with ease. Out in the hall, I put my hand against the knocker, and the door slowly eased back on its hinges before closing with a click and a lock.

Then I turned around and shut my eyes. In that moment, I could feel my consciousness reach out, farther beyond myself. And I could hear them: thousands upon thousands of little voices.

Come to me. The words called out from my mind, almost as loud as if I had spoken them. *Come to my aid.*

And I could hear them.

The rats.

Every rat in the castle, scampering and running as fast as they could to meet me.

Find my friends, I added. *Free them from their prison.*

A portion of the rising horde broke off and headed down to the dungeons.

As for myself, I turned back toward the giant door. And suddenly, my previous confusion was replaced with perfect clarity. I put my hand against the door, smiling a little. I hadn't gotten lost or confused on my way to the dungeons: it was the castle itself that brought me here.

I know the ends and outs of this castle like the back of my hand, and it knows me, bending to my every whim, opening doors to where I need to go, taking me to the places I need to be with a mere glimmer of thought....

I blinked rapidly and fell back a step. Again, I looked around for any signs that someone might have joined me, but there was no one. What a strange thing for me to think, especially since this was my first time ever in the castle!

Shrugging, I stepped back up to the door and laid my hand over the knocker.

'Where are you going now?' asked Windtail as she hopped up onto my shoulder.

I smiled.

"The throne room."

And with that, I gave the knocker a quick tug and pulled it open again.

On the other side was an enormous room made of black marble and, on the far side, a marble throne placed high on a dais.

'How did you do that?' Windtail gasped.

My smile faded. "Well, I guess I just...felt the magic and activated it."

And with that, I stepped through the door and into chaos.

Oh. *That's* where all the people went. Did *everyone* have a magic door to the throne room? Because that's sure what it felt like. Maids and servants, cooks and guards, all of them crowded together, an odd assortment of humans and elves, much too tall and self-absorbed to notice one little goblin stepping into the room. Or maybe it was because they all seemed so agitated, anxiously murmuring among themselves as they stood around.

"I say, you there! Goblin!"

I spun around to find a large, balding human marching toward me. His face was red, and he swiped a handkerchief over his brow.

"Where is the master?" he demanded. "We haven't seen hide nor hair of him since his summons!"

I shrugged. "I dunno. Who's your master?"

But before the man could answer, a door swung open on the far side of the room, and an enormous mountain troll filled the entire doorway.

"Jab!" I shouted.

I broke into a run. Humans and elves parted for me with gasps and cries of alarm, but I didn't care. I ran as fast as I could, then took the last few steps in one giant leap. I caught Jab around the middle in a hug, and the troll covered me with his hands in return.

"Jab!" I said again, relief washing over me. "You're alright!"

The troll gave a chuckling grunt and thumped me twice on the back, nearly knocking the air out of my lungs.

"Move out of the way, you great lump!"

Jab flinched and stepped around to the side, revealing a very haggard looking Kurz. The orc scowled when he caught sight of me.

"And just what have *you* been doing? Skulking in the shadows while we do all the dirty work?"

I just blinked at him. "Well...yeah? That's kinda the job Teagan hired me to do?"

Kurz's scowl deepened and he waved a hand in dismissal. "Voiding fool. Where's the captain, anyhow? I'm gonna throttle him with my bare—"

But at that moment, the doors banged open behind me, and I spun around to find none other than Captain Teagan standing in the doorway.

I gaped at him. "But...I watched you fall out of a window!"

Teagan's face contorted with rage as he marched toward me. "You!" he yelled. "You cost me *everything!*"

I sighed. Why did these powerful magic-users keep blaming me for their own incompetence?

"Where is it?" Teagan demanded, coming to a stop in front of me. He looked like he'd been chewed up a few times by a dragon—his clothes were ragged, his hair was a mess, and he looked oddly small now that he had no hat. "Where is the Seeing Stone?"

"Ask your elf friend," I scowled. "*He's* the one who stole it!"

Teagan growled in frustration and moved as if to grab me. I started to shrink back, but froze when Jab and Bash both stepped up on either side of me. Teagan glared at them.

"Back off, *now*," he said, his voice a deadly calm. "And I *might* let this slide."

I could tell Jab was nervous by the way his shoulders hunched. But he crossed his arms and stood his ground.

"You stupid monsters!" Teagan yelled. "You obey *me!*"

He threw out his hand, and I could feel the air ripple as he summoned his magic. I watched in horror as Jab, Bash, and all the rest of the crew cried out and fell to their knees, clutching at their necks as whip-like tendrils of dark-light sprouted from their slave brands. Anger bubbled up within me—a hot, consuming anger I'd never felt before.

"No!" I hissed, thrusting a finger toward the former captain. A feeling like lightning shot through my arm and out my hand, and the next thing I knew, Teagan was screaming in pain.

Then a horde of rats burst into the room, running together in a great cascade. The throne room erupted with shrieks of terror as many of the servants fled. And when the dust settled, Teagan was on his knees, completely covered in rats. He let out an awful shriek.

Panting, I turned back to my friends. "Jab are you all—"

I stopped, staring, as Jab rubbed his throat. The troll's eyes were wide, and when he lowered his hand, my mouth fell open.

His slave brand was gone.

"What in the Void is this?" Kurz hissed. My gaze snapped to him, where he too sat rubbing his skin, now free of the inky slave brand. He turned his incredulous gaze on me. "What did you do?"

The entire crew was doing the same, feeling their throats and looking at me in awe. I swallowed and looked down at my hands.

"I...I don't—"

A bellow tore through the air, and I jumped out of the way as Kurz leapt to his feet and ran straight past me.

Straight for Teagan.

With a swipe of his hand, he sent rats flying and pulled the captain up to his feet, drawing his arm back and landing a punch on Teagan's jaw.

"It's over, Teagan!" the orc snarled, punching him again, then again. "That's the last time you throw us to the wolves! You're dead! Do you hear me? *Dead!*"

"No!"

The word flew from my mouth before I realized what I was saying. Suddenly everyone was looking at me again, and I tried my best not to cower under their gaze. Even Kurz stood motionless, glaring back at me with his fist still raised.

I swallowed past the dry feeling in my throat. "Don't kill him, Kurz!"

"Give me one good reason why I shouldn't!" the orc snarled.

I licked my lips. Why *didn't* I want to kill Teagan? He certainly deserved it, but I couldn't explain how I didn't want us to become like him.

Because he can help us find my Seeing Stone.

The words came to me as if someone were whispering in my ear.

"Because he mentioned something about a Seeing Stone!" I blurted. "It's...it's very powerful and valuable, and I want a chance to find it!"

It felt like I was spouting off nonsense, and I knew Kurz would never agree. But to my surprise, the orc lowered his fist and dropped Teagan back into the mound of rats.

"Fine," he growled. "You broke my slave bond, so I owe you." He jabbed a finger in my direction. "But this is the only time we do things your way."

And with that, the orc turned and marched away, disappearing through the grand entry doors.

Teagan laughed, and I stared with disdain at the man before me. Blood dripped from his nose and stained his teeth as he grinned viciously.

"Just you wait, goblin!" he cried. "This isn't over! It's only a matter of time before someone bigger and smarter than you manages to steal that throne back! And when they do, I hope they hang you by your toes. I hope they exterminate every last rat on the face of the—"

The captain stopped, mouth still open. Because I was smiling. A wide, fiendish smile that showed off my large, pointed teeth.

Because the rats were gathering.

First a chirp, then a pattering of clawed feet. Then they were bursting through the windows, crawling under doors, throwing themselves between the feet of all the present bystanders.

"You wish to exterminate all the rats?" I asked.

The rats threw themselves down at my feet, piling one on top of the other. The mountain of rats grew, lifting me higher. Those around me backed away, until even Jab had to leave my side.

"Funny," I said, locking eyes with Teagan. "The thing about rats is that there're too many for you to kill. There are many of us—and only one of you."

The rats stopped their climbing, and I stood so high that, at long last, I was able to look down on the humans and elves that had always towered over me

I liked this new power. I liked it *a lot*. I didn't want to kill Teagan, but I *could* make him hurt, if I wanted to. Did I want to?

On my shoulder, Windtail placed a tiny claw on my neck. I looked at her, and her scarlet eyes bored into me. She didn't have to say a word.

I sighed. She was right of course. I didn't actually want to hurt Teagan either.

With a flick of my thoughts, I compelled the rats forward. One side of the mountain began to fall as the rats broke away, tumbling over each other as they ran and leapt toward the captain.

"Wait!" Teagan screamed, trying to scramble to his feet. "Wait, no—no!"

But he couldn't escape. One by one, the rats surrounded him, crawling over him, pinning his arms behind his back. They clung to him, digging their claws into his clothes, forming a new pile with Teagan at the very center, until all that could be seen of him was his head.

His screams split the air, long agonized shrieks of fear and pleas for mercy. They were horrible enough to turn anyone's blood to ice, and I decided very quickly that I was sick of the sound.

"Oh, shut up!" I shouted, and a large fat rat crawled over the captain's face and lay down over his mouth, stifling the scream. "Get a grip! I ain't gonna kill you! They're just gonna take you to the dungeons, is all!"

Teagan's eyes were wide and glossy. A gurgle escaped his throat as the rats hoisted him off the ground and carried him longways across the throne room. The captain gasped and struggled, but the rats held him fast, marching like little soldiers as they made their way to the dungeons.

As soon as Teagan was out of sight, I slumped, letting out a long sigh that felt heavy in my bones. I was passed from rat to rat, and they set me gently on the floor, where I stumbled a step before falling against something solid. When I looked, I saw that it was Jab holding me upright.

"Thank you, friend," I said, grateful. My heart was hammering painfully and my hands were shaking.

But it was over. Teagan could rot in the dungeons for all I cared. Maybe I'd interrogate him later, but right now I was just glad to be free of the human that had caused us so much pain.

Taking a deep breath, I dismissed the rats, and they began to disperse.

Jab poked me lightly on the head, his expression full of concern.

"Oh, I'm alright," I said. "I was so afraid he'd see right through me." I shivered and hugged myself. "I didn't *really* want to kill him, just scare him a little."

And make sure he never hurt me or Jab or anyone again.

"S-s-s-sir?"

My head snapped up, and I was surprised to see the same balding, red-faced human from before. I glanced over my shoulder, expecting to see some kind of war general or another wizard maybe. But there was no one else.

"Uh," I said, shifting from foot to foot. "Are you talking to me?"

"Indeed," the man answered. Sweat had gathered on his forehead again, which he hastily wiped away. "If I may ask, sir, what do you plan on doing with us?"

"Huh?"

I peered over his shoulder and saw that almost all of the servants had fled, though a few of the guards remained, looking a little uncertain as they watched us.

I blinked. "Uh, well, I hadn't planned on anything, really. I just wanted to get rid of Teagan. Who're you again?"

The man looked offended. "Why, I am James Mortimer, steward and head of staff here at Shadowmoor castle!"

"Oh, uh, alright?" Did that mean he was important?

"So...you weren't planning on feed *us* to your...um, *pets*, were you?"

"Why would I do that?" I asked. "You didn't hurt me." I narrowed my eyes. "Did you?"

"No, no!" Mor-Whats-His-Name said quickly. "Of course not! We only just met!" He took a tentative step forward, stooping slightly. "Pray tell me, where is the Lord Varyon?"

I frowned. "The what now?"

The steward was starting to get annoyed. "Dari Varyon—Lord of Shadowmoor!"

I shook my head. "Never heard of him."

The steward squinted at me. "The dark elf wizard? Surely you couldn't have missed him!"

"Ohhh!" I nodded importantly. "Yeah I saw that guy. He's dead."

A strange gleam came into the steward's eyes. "Dead?" he said quickly. "Are you quite sure?"

"Oh yeah. He was fighting Teagan and this other guy, Faerie Lord, who stabbed him, and then Teagan stole a rock from him, but then Faerie Lord stole the rock, so the wizard grabbed me and went up in a puff of black smoke."

"Good gracious!" The steward began to pace. "This is certainly a strange turn of events. Varyon...dead!" He turned and addressed the guards. "With Lord Varyon dead, I suppose there's no choice but for me to take charge!"

I stiffened, the wizard's words suddenly ringing through my head.

"Don't let the steward try and take control! The fate of this world—and the next—depends upon it!"

I scratched my ear, finding the words pretty pompous for a dead man. That said, there *was* something...*hungry* in the steward's eye that I didn't like.

"Uh, actually?" I said quickly. "The wizard left me in charge."

The steward froze mid-stride, nose wrinkling as he turned to look at me.

"Oh?" he said sharply. "Is that so?" He clasped his hands behind his back and looked me up and down, a sneer curling his lips. "The wizard lord Dari Varyon left *you* in charge of everything he owns? And what would give you an idea like that?"

My chest started to pound. How could I prove it?

The medallion, fool!

Huh, that was a pretty rude thing for me to think about myself. Nevertheless, I reached beneath my shirt and withdrew the shiny golden medallion with the ruby glimmering inside.

"Probably because he gave me this."

"The steward's eyes grew wide with anger, then with fear. "Th-the master's medallion?" He sounded more than a little upset. He glanced at the guards, who were all nodding and murmuring ascent. I had no idea what made this medallion so special, but I was *really* glad the wizard had given it to me.

The steward seemed about ready to explode. But, after some muttering, he looked down his nose at me.

"Very well," he sniffed. "All hail...what was your name again?"

I grinned. "Rat King!"

The steward's eyes rolled up to the ceiling. "All hail the Rat King, I suppose." Then he turned on his heel and left without another word.

For a moment we stood there in stunned silence as I realized that all that was left was Captain Teagan's former crew. Then one of them shouted, "Three cheers for Rat King!"

My face and ears burned with embarrassment as suddenly they were all shouting, "*Rat King! Rat King! Rat King!*"

Jab lifted me off the ground and deposited me on the throne. I settled back in the imposing chair and immediately hated it. This would definitely be the first thing to go. I liked the height though. I'd just find a better one.

'So,' said Windtail. *'What are we going to do now?'*

"Dunno," I answered, turning to look at Jab. He'd taken up position on the left side of my throne, and I was pleased to find Bash taking up the right. The two of them made quite the impressive bodyguards. "What do you guys want to do?"

Bash gave me a look of bewilderment, then shrugged, so I turned to Jab instead. My friend seemed lost in thought for a long moment, then nodded and patted his stomach twice.

"I s'pose you're right, Jab!" I said, standing up from the throne and adjusting my spectacular hat. "I *could* go for something to eat!"

As we all trooped out to raid the kitchens, I couldn't help but smile to myself. This adventure hadn't ended so badly after all! Who knew what would happen next?

Don't miss the next installment of Rat King's journey:

RAT KING
AND THE REIGN OF DARKNESS

Coming soon to a sewer near you!

About the Author

Olivia is a science fiction and fantasy author, whose greatest desire is to tell stories that bring light and hope to readers. Her love for robots and monsters leads her to write books that challenge stereotypes, while also providing clean content for readers of all ages. Olivia works as an art teacher and loves to spread the joy of creativity with her students. She lives in Oklahoma with her family, and when she isn't writing, can be found gaming, drinking tea, and making quirky, colorful art.

Find her on Instagram @oliviagratehouse or online at oliviagratehouse.com

Made in the USA
Columbia, SC
26 May 2025